MUST BE CLOWNING ME

Once Upon a Bite #3

Charity Parkerson

Punk & Sissy Publications

COPYRIGHT

—Warning: This book is intended for readers over the age of 18. Some of my books contain allusions to past abuse and trauma. I try to have nothing triggering on page and treat every situation with care.

Editor: BZ Hercules & Consultants

CONTENTS

INTRODUCTION

All Jake wants is a fresh start. He REALLY gets his wish. Now he's trapped for eternity as a night dweller.

Only Jake could get attacked by a vampire clown the moment he moves his therapy practice to New Orleans. Fortunately, the town is rife with supernatural clients to keep his business afloat. But life has always enjoyed a good laugh at Jake's expense, and he can't stop thinking about one client in particular. The vampire who found him and saved him.

Having a vampire therapist is a bit of a dream come true for Aaron. He's been needing one for a while. Aaron has a barrel full of issues to work out, and it's easier if his therapist knows about the supernatural world. Unfortunately, Aaron never expected his therapist to be so hot, and they have a connection from day one. There's no way for him to stay on task. Aaron doesn't know if he's getting better or if he's falling in love. Truthfully, he's also not sure if he cares anymore, as long as he gets to keep seeing Jake.

Must be Clowning Me is the third book in Charity Parkerson's Once Upon a Bite series. These books are meant to be short, fun paranormal romps to brighten your day.

CHAPTER ONE

A WARM BREEZE RATTLED the leaves. It was a nice night for a walk, even if it was only a short one before his first appointment in a new city. Jake had always wanted to live in a walkable neighborhood. When he had thought about that type of life, he had never considered New Orleans. It always seemed like much bigger or smaller places jumped to mind. A bell jingled, catching Jake off guard and pulling him from his thoughts. It seemed such an out-of-place sound—like one of those little balls at the end of a cat toy. The smallest of annoying jingles on an otherwise silent night. Jake checked behind him. There was nothing there. Just trees and empty sidewalk.

Jake shook his head and kept moving. Three months ago, he had moved his practice from Nashville to here. He had been ready for a change and the area had a shortage of therapists. It seemed like a good fit. He wanted to help. So far, he couldn't complain. He liked the weather and the walking. The bell sounded again. This time, a honk followed—like the horn on a kid's bike. Jake's heart jumped into his throat. He spun. No one was there. The sidewalk behind him was still empty. His gaze scanned the tree line of the nearby park. Nothing. Jake kept moving, but this time, his every sense stayed tuned in to his surroundings. He wasn't alone. The hair stood on the back of his neck. His senses heightened. With each step he took, Jake expected an attack from every corner. Maybe he watched too many horror movies or old childhood fears came back to haunt him. Either way, he knew the worst would come.

A rapid jingle rushed him. Jake spun and swept his leg, taking out the legs of the brightly dressed man running at him. A red wig went flying. Multiple horns squeaked as the guy hit the pavement. Hard. He honked as he landed.

"What the fuck, dude? What's wrong with you?"

Jake stared down at the clown on the ground. He was literally a clown. Face paint. Big red nose. Multi-colored patchwork outfit. The whole nine yards. He would have had a wig too if Jake hadn't attacked him.

The guy held his back as he rolled to his side, reaching for his fake red hair. "I'm running late for a party, or I'd call the cops, man."

Horror washed over Jake as he realized he had attacked some poor guy for no reason. He rushed to help the man to his feet. "I'm so sorry. You were running up on me and I thought..." Jake didn't know how to finish that sentence. He felt like an idiot.

"This is a public sidewalk, asshole. Other people are allowed to use it. I swear, one of these days, us clowns are going to come together and get justice for all the violence against us. We're just trying to live our lives. Next time, you might find yourself charged with a hate crime."

"I didn't even know you were a clown," Jake argued weakly as the clown stomped away in his big shoes, jingling down the sidewalk. With a shake of his head, Jake swiped a shaky hand over his eyes. He couldn't believe he had done something so insane. The guy had every right to call the police. Jake had attacked him from nowhere. While still recovering from the mortification, Jake resumed his walk. For the most part, he felt safe here in New Orleans. He supposed he let some of the lore get to him occasionally. Plus, it was dark and the homeless could be very aggressive. Still, this was definitely one of those moments Jake would wake up in the middle of the night thinking about in ten years and still feel the embarrassment. He cringed. His ex would love using this as an example of his paranoia. It didn't matter Malachi had been gaslighting him the entire time they had been dating. There was nothing Malachi loved more than a cruel laugh at Jake's expense. Bells jingled in the distance again. This time, Jake didn't look. He wouldn't get accused of some fucked-up form of clown bigotry again. Not twice in one night. He honestly didn't have any love for clowns, but he also didn't normally slam them to the ground on sight. A sinister laugh rippled through the air. The hair stood on the back of Jake's neck again.

"Hey, you." The teeny voice had Jake bracing himself against what he would see when he turned. He expected his worst nightmares come to life. There was nothing. The world went black.

A loud heartbeat pounded in Jake's ears. Copper filled his mouth.

"I thought your days of turning people against their will were behind you."

The voice seemed to come from miles away, yet right next to him. Nothing made sense.

"I didn't turn him. He was like this when I found him. I swear." Damn. That voice was nice.

"What's that all over him? It looks like smeared makeup, but not regular make-up. It's too shiny and white."

Jake tried to pry open his eyes. Everything was too bright. He was inside, but he didn't know where. Three men hovered over him, looking like concerned angels. Despite the assault on his senses, Jake still felt safe.

"What's wrong with me?" The words croaked from Jake's sore throat.

The three men exchanged glances. The only dark-haired one answered. "I'm sorry. You've been turned into a vampire."

Jake blinked, hoping to make the words make sense. The terrifying image of a six-foot clown with razor-sharp teeth floated across his mind. A vague memory of fangs sinking into his throat rose to the surface. Jake was too exhausted to feel much of anything other than a vague sense of disconnection from reality. "You must be clowning me."

The younger of the two blonds snapped his fingers. “That’s it. It’s clown makeup.”

Jake passed out again.

CHAPTER TWO

HE WAS THE MOST beautiful man Aaron had ever set eyes on, and Aaron felt super guilty for ogling him while he slept. Aaron had checked the guy's wallet after finding him on the sidewalk. Since he had turned an unfortunate number of humans on accident after he had been forcibly turned—thanks to finding feeding awkward—Aaron had known immediately what happened. Jake Romans was thirty-two. Six foot one with dark blue eyes. He lived across town. Aaron didn't know why he had been out walking late at night, but it hadn't gone well for him. He also didn't know why the guy had been covered in clown makeup, unless he was into some weird fetish shit. If so, Aaron wouldn't judge. Aaron enjoyed hanging out at a certain club downtown for some specific tastes. It was freeing. He didn't have to hide his vampirism there. No one thought it was real. Still, Aaron desperately wanted Jake to open his eyes again. He had only been awake for half a minute earlier in the night. Aaron hadn't been able to stay away since.

"It wasn't a bad dream."

A smile automatically snapped to Aaron's lips at Jake's disgruntled tone. He forced it away. "No. I'm sorry."

Dark blue eyes focused on him. "What's your name?"

"Aaron."

"You saved me."

It hadn't been a question, but Aaron still nodded. It wasn't often he got to play the hero. Usually, he was the bad guy. "I'm glad I came along when I did. A normal person would've taken you to the hospital. They would've given you a blood infusion, which likely would've killed you. Bagged blood is too filtered. We can't really survive on that, especially a new turn." Aaron felt the panic growing inside Jake.

Calm down. Breathe. You're a professional. You can handle this.

At Jake's loud and raging thoughts, Aaron took his hand. "Breathe."

Damn. He has nice hands. Stop. He's way too young for you. You can't even keep a man your own age. Plus, you're having an existential crisis right now.

Aaron bit his lip to keep from smiling. He didn't want to embarrass Jake by letting him know he could hear his thoughts. "What do you do for work?" Aaron asked instead, hoping to distract him.

"I'm a therapist. Shit. Sorry. I had an appointment with a client tonight."

Aaron's eyebrows rose. "You're joking. Wait." He released Jake's hand and stood. After digging out his phone from his pocket, he clicked around and checked the details of his appointment. “What are the odds?”

“What?”

Aaron turned his phone so Jake could see his calendar. “I was your appointment tonight. That explains why we were both in the same area around the same time. If I wasn’t notoriously bad at remembering people’s names, I might’ve realized sooner, but...” Aaron shrugged.

Jake pushed himself into a sitting position and leaned back against the headboard. He glanced down. “My shirt is gone.”

Aaron’s gaze moved to Jake’s chest. It was a really nice chest. Firm. Hairy. “It was covered in blood and makeup.”

“Well.” Jake cleared his throat and squared his shoulders. “If you can pretend I'm not half dressed, let's have your first session now. I could use the distraction."

An uncomfortable-sounding laugh burst from Aaron. "Um. Sure. Okay. I'm Aaron. Nice to meet you."

A sexy smile stretched Jake's lips. "Hi, Aaron. I'm Jake. Why don't you tell me a little about yourself?"

Aaron swiped his sweaty palms down his thighs. "Sure. Technically speaking, I'm nineteen, about to be twenty."

"Technically speaking?"

Aaron nodded. "I got turned into a vampire when I was seventeen, so I'm pretty much trapped in a seventeen-year-old body, but I was born nineteen years ago, so I'm nineteen."

Jake nodded.

Aaron continued. "I still live with my dad and stepdad." He shrugged, feeling uncomfortable as hell. "The three of us just go together. Plus, we work together on my stepdad's spin class subscription service. I handle the tech side of everything. You know, the video editing, uploading and all that. We're a pack. I don't know. We fit."

"You don't have to justify staying in a safe and happy home."

Aaron flashed Jake a grateful smile. He felt a bit like a loser explaining to someone like Jake that he wasn't ready to go it alone. Most of that had to do with being a vampire. He was terrified of himself and their kind. His maker had already tried to murder his dad. They were safer together.

"Tell me about your dads."

Aaron winced. "My dad, Vega, he's my real dad. I was born by surrogate and he's my actual dad. You know, his DNA. Anyhow, his first husband, Terry, adopted me, and they raised me together. They were my parents. I called them Dad and Daddy T. I thought we were the perfect family. When I was fifteen, Daddy T asked me to stop calling him that. He said it made him uncomfortable. That should've been my first clue he didn't want me anymore. Six months later, he skipped out, leaving us for this guy who had just turned eighteen. He never looked back." Aaron fought the urge to rub his chest, even though he realized now how big of a piece of shit Terry was. Terry had been messing with a guy he really had no business at all messing with. Not only that, but he left a whole family for him. Still, that had been his dad. Aaron lost a dad. It hurt.

Aaron took a breath. He didn't want to cry. "Anyhow, I started acting out after he left. Going out and hanging out in places I shouldn't be. That's how I ended getting turned. To make a long story short, I accidentally turned my now stepdad, and that's how he met my dad. They fell in love, and he's been ten times the man Terry ever was. He's the one who convinced me to find a therapist. So, that's me, I guess."

A bright smile lit Jake's face. "That's not you. That's a highlight reel. You are your favorite video games. The moments you spend with your family. You are the funny faces you make at yourself in the mirror when no one else is around. The pep talks you give yourself before you do something you think you're too scared to do. Your thoughts and desires. People are so much more than a handful of ugly moments. You choose what defines you."

Aaron had never been so instantly fascinated by anyone. He couldn't explain it. Maybe it was because he had saved Jake or because he was half dressed. Possibly it was because he had just spilled his heart out to him. Aaron didn't really understand the whys, but he didn't want Jake to leave. He was surprisingly comfortable baring his soul. It felt right when they were together.

Each moment Jake spent with Aaron, the more normal he felt. Unfortunately, the knowledge he was now a vampire, and he knew nothing about that, still lived in the back of his brain every second they spoke. He kept waiting for the moment the panic would rise and take hold. It was only a matter of time. Jake was a man of action. He liked to have a plan. Not knowing what he faced was the worst part.

"This is going better than I expected. I'm glad I let Cosmos talk me into therapy."

Jake forced his mind to stay on track. "Cosmos is your stepdad, right?"

"Right. He owns Cosmic Cardio downtown. That's the subscription service I help him with. He records his spin classes and I—"

Jake's teeth chattered. He snapped them together. "Sorry."

A sympathetic smile touched Aaron's lips. "It's okay. You're doing great. When I turned, I didn't know a single vampire. In fact, I didn't think they existed. So, I just had to come home and find out for myself what my life would be like. It was a nightmare. You have us, so you don't have to go through anything alone. If you have a question, just ask." Aaron started, as if he recalled something important. "Oh, you should probably feed now that you're awake. Dad or Cosmos will have to show you how."

Jake's gaze slid toward the closed bedroom door. It occurred to him he hadn't truly looked away from Aaron's face since he opened his eyes. He was in a small bedroom. Everything was clean with neutral colors. It looked like a guest bedroom that never got used. Jake's gaze immediately returned to where he felt safe, holding the light green stare of the blond at his bedside. "Why can't you show me?"

A blush touched Aaron's cheeks. It was adorable. Jake's stomach growled. "Um. I don't... I've never been very comfortable with the whole feeding aspect of vampirism. In fact, it's caused me a lot of problems. You'd just be better off with someone else."

Jake was a therapist all the way to his soul. He needed to know more. He always had to dig deeper, picking at every wound. “Is there a certain part of feeding that makes you more uncomfortable than the rest, or is it the entire experience?”

Aaron scratched the side of his nose and looked away. It was obvious Jake had touched a nerve. “It’s not really something I can explain if you haven’t experienced it.”

“So let’s do this, and then I’ll know. I can’t help if I don’t understand.”

Aaron met and held his stare. He didn’t respond.

“I’m your therapist. You’re safe with me.”

“If I...” Aaron cleared his throat. He tried again. “My issues are mine. So if you’ll let Cosmos or Dad feed you, then yes. I'll show you."

Jake nodded and climbed from the bed. He expected to be unsteady. Aaron must have expected the same, because he rushed to hold Jake upright. Regretfully, Jake was fine to stand on his own. He still didn't get in a hurry to move from Aaron's hold. Aaron was small and beautiful. He was angelic-looking. Jake had a terrible time tearing his eyes away from him.

The dark-haired vampire came through the door, saving Jake from himself. "You're up. I was just coming to talk to you about learning how to feed."

Jake smiled. "Aaron was just bringing me to you for the same reason."

“This is Cosmos,” Aaron said, saving Jake from having to ask.

Cosmos smiled. He looked nice. He had the lightest blue eyes Jake had ever seen. They were almost unnatural. “Are you ready?”

“Not really,” Jake answered honestly.

“I get it, but life sucks sometimes.”

A smile snapped to Jake’s lips. Cosmos was obviously the no-nonsense type. He didn’t look like he put up with a lot of shit. It was no wonder Aaron liked him. Likely, Cosmos’ straightforward attitude was refreshing after having a parent leave him and not look back.

Jake straightened his spine. “Tell me what to do.”

Cosmos held out his arm. "Do you hear my pulse?"

Jake focused on Cosmos' wrist. He heard his heartbeat. "Yes."

"Good. Follow your instincts."

Jake took Cosmos' arm and moved closer. His gums itched. He swore his teeth grew. Before he understood what happened, he latched on to Cosmos' wrist and sucked. Blood filled his mouth. His first reaction was to gag, but then Aaron rubbed his back. He relaxed and swallowed.

"Keep listening to my heartbeat. You'll know when to stop."

Jake didn't know what that meant, but then he heard it. Cosmos' heartbeat changed slightly. Jake stopped sucking.

"Good job. Now lick the wound closed." Jake did as told. When he pulled away, two puncture wounds slowly vanished. "And you have it. If you need to feed from a human, you'll have to take control of their mind first. You have time to learn that later, though."

Panic tried overtaking Jake again. There were too many things he didn't understand.

Aaron stroked his back again. "Don't worry. I'll show you. For now, you should go back to bed. I know you're not tired, but you've had a mentally exhausting day."

Jake let Aaron lead him back to bed as Cosmos left them alone again. Even though Jake didn't really need the help, he enjoyed being cared for in his time of need. Physically, he felt fine. But Aaron was right. Mentally, he was a mess.

"If you don't feel up to me holding up my end of the bargain tonight, I completely understand. It's not like we won't see each other again."

Jake latched on to the lifeline. "No. Please. I need the distraction." He held his arm out to Aaron the way Cosmos had done for him.

With a nod, Aaron moved to the bed and sat at Jake's hip. He took Jake's arm. Jake couldn't look away as Aaron licked his lips. The way he stared at Jake's arm made Jake's skin tingle. His heart raced. Then Aaron's lips touched his pulse point. Jake's dick went hard. He gasped. Jake tried swallowing the sound, but then Aaron's fangs buried into his skin and Jake saw stars. He moaned. His stomach muscles clenched. Each pull of blood from his body was like Aaron sucked hard on his cock. Jake clutched the covers, dug his heels into the mattress, and fought not to lift his hips to get deeper down an invisible throat. Aaron kept sucking and Jake kept shamelessly moaning like he filmed a porn scene. He had no control. Then Aaron licked his wrist and jets of cum filled Jake's underwear while Jake gasped uncontrollably in a heap against the headboard. He stared at Aaron in total shock as Aaron panted beside him. Aaron turned his head. Their gazes met. Jake almost came again. No one had ever looked at him with more hunger.

"I can't be your therapist."

Aaron blinked. His expression turned sad. He nodded. “That’s fair.” He stroked Jake’s wrist one final time before releasing his arm. “I’m broken beyond repair.”

Horror overcame Jake. “No. Why would you say that? I can’t be your therapist and be sexually attracted to you.”

“Oh.” Aaron didn’t sound relieved. “Are you sure that you are? I think it’s just the way I feed. You wanted me to show you. None of that happened when you bit Cosmos. But this is why feeding is uncomfortable for me. It’s extremely sexual.”

“Oh.” Jake blinked. He felt dumb. Obviously, he was sexually attracted to Aaron because he had been before Aaron bit him, but Aaron was only turned on from biting him. Now things were awkward.

Thankfully, Jake thrived in uncomfortable situations. "Um, well, how about I make you a counteroffer? I don't feel comfortable being your therapist after you made me come in my jeans."

"Did I?" Aaron looked his way with a bright smile.

Jake cleared his throat and pretended he hadn't heard Aaron's question. "And I need your help to learn the ins and outs of being a vampire, so how about we help each other? You can keep talking to me as if I'm your paid therapist and you can show me the ropes of being a vampire."

Aaron's gaze moved down Jake's body. "Do you like ropes?"

"Jesus, you're practically a child."

A bright smile snapped to Aaron's lips at Jake's muttered words. "Maybe, but do you know where vampires fit in best in New Orleans?" He didn't wait for Jake to guess. "The Rabbit Hole. It's a lifestyle club downtown. You should check it out with me sometime. People think everything there is a game. You don't have to hide your fangs." He held Jake's gaze, making Jake pant at the immediate images that filled his head. "You don't have to hide anything. Do you need me to lick up the mess I made?"

"Yes. No." Jake shook his head. "No. Oh my God."

An evil-sounding chuckle rumbled from Aaron as he stood. He waved his hand and a stack of clean clothes appeared at the foot of the bed. "There's a bathroom through that door." He motioned to the left. "I'll let you get some rest. If you need me... or if you just want me, think my name. I can hear your every thought. I'll come to you. Yes, I want you too. No, you're not too old for me. And no, I definitely don't want you only because I bit you. I've been watching you sleep and lusting after you." For a moment Aaron held Jake's gaze with such confidence, Jake almost begged him to stay. Aaron smirked. "You should definitely think my name later. I'll be worth it." With that promise lingering between them, Aaron left him alone and panting. Jake had no idea what happened to his life in the last twenty-four hours, but he wasn't sure all of it was bad. In fact, the sticky mess inside his underwear and the heat in his cheeks said he might be having the time of his life. How fucked up was that?

Chapter Three

For the tenth time, Jake straightened his shirt, making sure it was wrinkle-free. He already knew it was, but he couldn't stop. This first appointment with Aaron—after basically sneaking away in the middle of the night—was really playing hell on his nerves. He hadn't expected to learn Aaron could read his mind. That had been the real kicker. Each time he recalled every inappropriate thought he had about Aaron, he wanted the floor to swallow him whole all over again. Normally, he wasn't one to flinch easily, but he was used to hiding behind a mask of professionalism. If Aaron could see inside his head, he no longer had that protection, and Jake didn't know how to handle that. He kept reminding himself he wasn't Aaron's therapist. Not officially. At least he had done the right thing and immediately said he couldn't take Aaron as a client when he recognized he couldn't control his attraction to Aaron. Still, Jake agreed to keep seeing him, and what the fuck had he been thinking? He was way too old for Aaron.

His doorbell rang, and Jake took a shaky-sounding breath. He straightened his shirt again and headed for the door. His fangs grew and Jake had to force them back in before answering. He felt

Aaron on the other side. Heard his heart beating. Jake closed his eyes and savored the sound for a moment before finally opening the door. His breath caught without warning. Aaron looked gorgeous. He wore all black. His light hair and eyes seemed twice as eye-catching with the lack of color in his clothing. His gaze made a subtle sweep of Jake's body. A ridiculously confident smirk stretched his lips.

"Hey."

God help him. Jake's knees weakened. "Hey."

They stared at each other.

Aaron's smile grew. "Do I get to come inside?"

"Oh." Jake blushed as he stepped aside, making room for Aaron to pass. He inhaled as Aaron came within inches of him. *Why do you smell like apples?*

Aaron's head turned. Their gazes met. "Taste me and find out."

Until Aaron said the words aloud, Jake hadn't realized he had projected the question to Aaron. His hand moved to his stomach without thinking. He wanted Aaron. Jake was old enough to admit it. But he was wise enough to know better than to act on his every desire. "Would you like some water before we get started?"

"I don't drink water any longer, but thank you."

Jake fought the urge to smack his forehead. "Sorry. It's a habit I probably won't break anytime soon." He closed the door and motioned for Aaron to follow him. Jake spoke over his shoulder as he headed for the couch. "How has everything been since we last talked?"

A sexy chuckle nearly took out Jake's knees again. "It's only been twenty-four hours. Not much has happened with me. What about you? How are you holding up with your new life?"

Jake hadn't expected the conversation to turn to him. He made a dismissive gesture. "I'm still adjusting, so I'm not sure how to answer that yet. Thankfully, when I moved to New Orleans last month, I was immediately hit with nighttime bookings and barely any daytime inquiries, so there's that. At least I'm not worrying about my job."

They sat together on the couch and turned each other's way. Aaron genuinely cared. Jake felt that emotion vibrating from him. It was odd to know how other people truly felt now. That would definitely help in his line of work.

"I'm glad you won't be lacking in clients. They're probably all vampires who've been waiting for someone who would see them after sunset—like me. That's why I booked with you. No one else sees people after dark here."

"Really?" Obviously, Jake hadn't known vampires existed when he moved to New Orleans, but still. He couldn't believe a town this big didn't have a therapist willing to see clients when it was most convenient. A majority of people worked during the day and couldn't afford to take off for therapy sessions. Now he knew vampires existed, and Jake saw a whole community of neglected mental health. He hoped he could help.

"You're amazing."

Jake blinked, realizing he had gotten lost in his thoughts. "Sorry."

Aaron shook his head. "Don't apologize. I like listening to you think." He smiled. "Don't get upset. I can't control it. You'll have to learn how to block your thoughts. Right now, it's like you're speaking every thought out loud."

A blush exploded across Jake's face. He couldn't think of anything more horrific. "Um. Well. Maybe we should get started, then." He took a breath and tried to clear his mind of anything other than working. "Last night, we talked about your dads. Tonight, why don't you tell me about when you were turned?"

Aaron's smile slipped away. "Wow. Jumping into the deep end of the pool already. Okay." He cleared his throat. His light green gaze seemed to turn inward. "Let's see. Like I said, I was seventeen. My friend, Stephen, talked me into going to this party. He said it was at his cousin's house and their parents were out of town. Supposedly, it would only be a few people, but they had a pool and there would be beer. I was in a big rebellious stage since my dad had left about a year earlier, so I was all in. Then we got there, and the house was in this really sketchy neighborhood. There was no pool. Stephen claimed the party had been moved because his cousin got busted or whatever. I didn't care. I was seventeen. Of course, I thought I was invincible."

Jake smiled at the way Aaron spoke, as if seventeen had been a lifetime ago.

Aaron leveled a serious look at him. "It was. You're a vampire now. We'll live forever. Everyone and everything you've ever known is completely insignificant now. One day soon, it'll all be dust, but you and I will still be here. We're eternal. I can't explain how it changes you, but—eventually—it does. You don't feel the same about things that are fleeting and you find yourself holding on with both hands to things that you know will last. Those become the only things that truly matter any longer. That night, I couldn't wait to grow up. Hell, I thought I was already grown. I couldn't wait to move out of my dad's house and never look back. Now, I don't even think about leaving. They expect me to stay until I meet my soulmate because all we have that matters is each other." Aaron blinked, as if he realized how intense he had become during his speech. "You're hungry. Why haven't you fed tonight?"

Something unnamed grew inside Jake's chest. Aaron was wonderful. "I don't know how to control minds yet and I've been afraid to try."

Aaron stood. "Come on. You can't work under these conditions. Let me teach you how to use your mind control and have a little fun at the same time."

Jake didn't budge. "We haven't finished our session, and what about you? Have you fed tonight? I know you don't like to bite anyone."

Aaron's gaze moved down Jake's body, making every inch of him burn before returning to hold Jake's stare. "I enjoyed biting you."

You didn't answer my question.

"Would you be jealous if I bit someone else? Knowing how it makes me feel?"

Fuck. Why would he be jealous? He had no right. "Yes."

Aaron didn't smirk or gloat. That was the only thing saving Jake's pride. "Then come with me. Let me teach you how to get the blood you need so you can be the only one who feeds me."

The sheer possessiveness that stirred inside him at Aaron's words shocked Jake to his core. One of the biggest reasons he was still single was his refusal to be the least bit unhealthy in a relationship. The first red flag in any relationship after his nightmare relationship with Malachi, and he was gone. Everything about Aaron and him was a bright red sheet in front of a raging bull, and Jake stood still, waiting to get gored. He let Aaron pull him to his feet. Then he didn't let go when Aaron linked fingers with him. Hand in hand, they headed out.

"Do you trust me?"

"Of course." Jake meant it. There was just something about Aaron. He knew he was safe as long as Aaron had him.

Aaron nodded. "Then close your eyes."

Jake did as told. The air changed. Wind whipped across his skin as if a rapid ocean breeze overcame them.

"Okay. Let's go."

Jake opened his eyes, and they were in a back alley. His heart skipped a beat. He didn't know how they had gone from one place to another in a flash. "How did you do that? Where are we?"

Aaron held his hand and circled the building, speaking over his shoulder as he went. "Your powers are as deep and limitless as you let them be. I discovered a while back, if I wanted to be somewhere badly enough, I could be." They stopped outside a metal door. Aaron typed in a code, and the light on the keypad turned green. He pulled the door open and motioned Jake inside. Jake froze inside the doorway. Music poured out. The first sight that met him was a leather daddy checking IDs, but that wasn't what caught and held Jake's attention. There was a guy getting blown literally three feet from the door.

"IDs and membership cards."

Aaron held up his empty palm.

The leather daddy stared at Aaron's hand a moment. "Okay. You two have fun."

Jake blinked.

Aaron pulled Jake deeper into the building. He yelled close to Jake's ear to be heard over the music. "This is The Rabbit Hole. It's an exclusive anything goes kink club. This is the perfect place to learn to use your powers because—if you fail—people will just think vampirism is your kink."

That made sense.

Aaron pulled him onto the dance floor. "Dance with me."

Jake didn't recognize the music, but he didn't hear it anymore once his body met Aaron's. Their skin met and moved against each other. Jake forgot to focus on anything else. Aaron held his stare.

Pick your meal.

The thought brushed his brain, bringing him back to reality. This wasn't about his lust. He needed to eat.

Aaron's mouth touched his ear. "This is very much about lust. The faster you eat, the quicker I can sink my fangs into you. I want to be inside you."

Damn. Everything about him was sexual, and Jake didn't know how to handle it. Yet his gaze skimmed the crowd, obeying Aaron's demands. As he searched for his dinner, Aaron's hands roamed his body, making him hard. The shirt he had been so worried about earlier slowly unbuttoned until the two halves parted. Warm lips touched his chest. Jake panted. His fangs grew. A slight glimpse of a man caught his attention. He looked familiar, but he disappeared before Jake got a good look at him. A woman caught his stare and the strange moment of uncomfortable familiarity passed.

Come to me.

Jake didn't think about it. He simply commanded her to obey.

She headed his way. As she reached their sides, Jake continued holding her stare while Aaron kept exploring his chest.

Give me your wrist. I need your blood.

She held out her wrist.

Jake took her hand, lowered his head, and bit. She moaned. He focused on holding on to her mind and listening to her heartbeat. The slight shift happened, and he retracted his fangs, licking the wound closed.

Thank you. Go away.

She walked away, leaving them alone.

Aaron kissed his neck. *Good job.* His fangs sank into Jake's throat. Jake's knees weakened. His dick twitched, but he managed not to immediately come this time. Jake's head spun. Aaron withdrew his fangs and his mouth covered Jake's. Their tongues met and stroked. Aaron's hands roamed inside Jake's open shirt, toying with his nipples and chest hair. Jake couldn't think. All he could do was feel. Aaron was an intense person. His emotions overwhelmed Jake's. Until that moment, Jake hadn't realized how much life he missed by watching from the sidelines. He had his reasons for going into this line of work. Jake protected himself with his education and career, but goddamn. For the first time, Aaron made him want all the things he feared.

Say you want me.

"I want you," Jake whispered against Aaron's lips.

Wind whipped around them, and the music disappeared. Jake tore his mouth away. He had to know where Aaron had taken them. They stood in the middle of Jake's bedroom, and they were already nude. He was blown away by Aaron's power. Aaron could do anything. It was almost terrifying, but scared wasn't how he felt at that moment. Jake only needed one thing. For once, there was nothing standing in his way.

It had been risky, taking Jake straight to his bedroom and removing all obstacles. Aaron had asked. That didn't mean Jake understood what he agreed to since Jake was only newly turned. He didn't know how much he could do yet. Aaron held his breath as he watched Jake eye his surroundings and then their nudity. Heat flashed in his eyes.

"Good." He came back at Aaron with every bit as much force as he had in the club.

Aaron moaned as their tongues met. Jake was hungry. Aaron felt that one emotion above all others. He had either been neglected or repressed. Possibly both. Either way, he didn't hold back with Aaron. All his usual thoughts about Aaron being too young for him were gone. Jake touched him. Aaron savored every second. He didn't feel like anyone touched him willingly anymore. Everything was about blood and mind control. Jake genuinely wanted him. The knowledge had him choking back emotions.

"Tell me how you want me. I can't read you the way you can read me."

Aaron experienced a moment of unexpected panic. "I don't bottom."

Jake kissed his cheek and neck before swiping a quick kiss across his lips. He was so gentle. "That's fine. I'm vers, so whatever you need is good with me."

Aaron's shoulders relaxed. He released the breath he hadn't known he had been holding. Unfortunately, it sounded shaky on the way out. Jake didn't call him on it. He simply whisked his lips across Aaron's again before turning away.

Aaron watched, drunk on lust, as Jake turned down the bedcovers and then slid open the bedside drawer. He found lube and a condom.

A smile snapped to Aaron's lips. "We are technically the undead, angel. We can't get or spread disease."

Jake froze. He dropped his gaze to the foil package he held. "Oh." He tossed it back in the drawer. With lube in hand, he crawled onto the mattress, giving Aaron a sexy show. Aaron's stomach growled. No one had ever made him so hungry. He didn't know it was possible to feel this way, especially so quickly after meeting someone. But all of Jake's mind was open to Aaron, and it was beautiful. He was smart and so fucking kind. Aaron had never met anyone like him before. He cared.

Jake settled on his back. He shook the lube at Aaron. "Do you plan to watch or participate? I can handle both."

He was fun. Aaron dove into bed. He tongued Jake's nipple while he lubed his asshole, going all in. Aaron let Jake's thoughts guide him. He was so focused, he couldn't tell any longer if Jake's moans and gasps were internal or aloud. It didn't matter, as long as Jake burned for him. Jake writhed beneath him as Aaron fingered his hole, getting him ready. He didn't want to hurt him.

"Fuck me already. Goddamn."

A chuckle that sounded evil even to Aaron burst from him at Jake's irritation. He positioned his cock against the tight ring of muscles surrounding Jake's asshole. His greedy hole tried sucking him deeper as Aaron pushed his way inside. Aaron gasped at the sensation. Jake was so hot and tight. Aaron had to pause and take a breath to keep from immediately blowing.

"Oh, my God. Feels so good. It's been so long since anything other than toys have been in my ass. Did I say that out loud?"

Aaron smiled. "It wouldn't have mattered. I would've heard it anyway."

"That's humiliating."

Aaron stopped mid-thrust and held Jake's stare. "You're not allowed to feel that way with me." He went root deep, making Jake gasp. "I'm inside your asshole. It doesn't get more personal than that." He pulled out slightly and thrust again, ensuring he hit at the angle he knew Jake liked. "We're past embarrassment. Tell me what else has been here, getting you off before I came along.

Were you using the normal dildos or do you like something darker?" Aaron kept thrusting while holding Jake's stare. He refused to let Jake hide. "Maybe you have alien shaped toys or you like stuffies. Don't leave anything out."

"I'm boring."

Aaron's gaze moved down Jake's body. His thick cock bounced with Aaron's every thrust, leaking pre-cum on to his stomach. An image invaded Aaron's mind of Jake in the shower. A thick dildo suction cupped to the wall while he fucked it. His head was thrown back. Water ran down his body while he rode the fake dick just the way he wanted.

"Goddamn, gorgeous. That's hot as hell. I'd pay good money to see that in real time." He leaned forward and pressed his forehead against Jake's and thrust into him. "But have you tried this one?" He projected an image of him fucking a vacuum hose, getting sucked off by the suction.

Jake cried out. Hot cum hit Aaron's chest. Jake's asshole tightened on him, trying to break him in two as his body tried sucking him deeper. Aaron gasped and shook. An orgasm rocked his soul. He cried out against Jake's skin as he pumped Jake's ass full of cum. Possessiveness roared through him. He had taken Jake's blood earlier and now he gave Jake his cum. It was as if life came full circle and some ritual he hadn't known about had taken place. Jake felt like he belonged to Aaron. He had never so desperately wanted to keep someone in all his life. Then, while the storm still raged inside him, Jake kissed him. It was a sweet, searching kiss. Their tongues played as their bodies floated through a cloud of ecstasy. They held each other and came down from the high together. Even after Aaron rolled to one side, they held and petted each other. Aaron had never felt closer to anyone. There was a level of intimacy between them he hadn't expected. Jake kept kissing the tip of his nose and forehead. Aaron couldn't stop smiling each time he did. It was like they were in a cocoon of happiness nothing could ruin.

"Tell me about the night you turned," Jake whispered in the dark.

Aaron was wrong. Something could ruin it. He didn't respond.

Jake kissed the tip of his nose again. "You didn't finish your story earlier. I think it's important."

Aaron took a breath. He wanted to give Jake everything, even this. "There's not a lot to tell because I don't really know. We got to this pretty nonexistent party. There was this guy there, and he started talking to me. After that, everything gets hazy. I woke up in an abandoned house in a different neighborhood the next night." Aaron took a shaky breath. "My body was completely healed, but I knew it had been—" Jake pressed his fingertips to Aaron's lips, stopping him.

"I'm hurting you. I'm trying to help, but this is hurting you."

Despite everything, Aaron smiled. He kissed Jake's fingers before pushing them away. "You feel what I do."

It hadn't been a question, but Jake nodded. "I want to help, but I'm not."

"You're not my therapist," Aaron reminded him.

A wave of sadness rolled from Jake. "You sought me out to get help."

Aaron moved closer and held Jake tighter. "I sought you out on Cosmos' advice. Not because I was driven by some great need to get help. But what I found is so much better than what I went looking for, and I'm not sorry." He pressed his forehead against Jake's. "And you're wrong. You have helped me. I hated feeding. It was something I always put off longer than I should because it didn't feel right. It feels right with you. I feel right when I'm with you."

Jake closed his eyes. He took a breath. "You're too amazing for your age."

A laugh burst from Aaron. "Stop." He pinned Jake to the bed and claimed his mouth. *I'll show you what I can do with all this youth. I can fuck you until the sun comes up.* He would too. Just to spite Jake. And because he couldn't get enough of the sexy body beneath him. He had never been happier. Aaron would make sure Jake felt the same. Jake didn't see it yet, but he was stuck with Aaron. Aaron felt something and he wouldn't let up until he figured out what. They may as well enjoy the ride.

Chapter Four

If Jake looked at things too closely, and circumstances had been different, he might have broken. Being attacked and turned against his will, it was horrific. His old life was lost to him. He could never step foot into the sun again. But there was another side to things. A silver lining. Jake had always been too optimistic for his own good, and—truth be told—he had always been more of a night owl anyhow. That was one of the biggest reasons he decided to work nights when he opened his practice. It was a win-win. His clients didn't have to miss work, and he got to sleep in. Now, rather than sleeping late, he slept all day. It wasn't like he had to force it. He conked out the moment the sun rose, and his eyes shot open the instant it set. Jake had never felt better and more well-rested in his life.

Then there was Aaron. Jake tried not to think too much about that. He was happier than he had ever been in his entire life. Jake never expected to feel so close to someone so quickly. Just over nine weeks since his attack had passed. They consisted of sixty-five of the steamiest nights of his life. He actually blushed sometimes thinking about it. Jake was older. He should be the kinkier of the two. No. Aaron never ran out of ideas. But it was the nights when Aaron made slow love to him while holding his stare. Those were the nights Jake felt exposed in a way he couldn't explain. Aaron saw his soul, and he didn't flinch.

The doorbell rang, signaling the arrival of Jake's next appointment and an end to his overthinking. As always, he needed to set Aaron aside while he worked. But truth be told, Jake never set Aaron aside for long and that was something he would need to face soon. When Jake opened the door, his mind blanked. He knew the face on the other side.

"Oh."

A bright smile stretched Malachi's lips. "Hey."

Jake blinked. He checked his notes. Fuck. There was no first name listed on the new client form he had just printed, only a letter. M. Stanford. Jake hadn't even checked the name. If he had, he would have immediately suspected Malachi was back to his old stalking ways. But Jake was in a new town. This couldn't be happening. "Malachi. This is unexpected."

"Yeah. I know. It's been a while. I couldn't believe it when I saw your name listed when I went searching for a therapist. When did you move to town?"

Jake took a step back, silently inviting Malachi inside. He didn't know why. His feet just moved. He hadn't told them to do so. They just did.

Malachi stepped inside and looked around. “This is a nice place. What made you leave Nashville?”

Jake closed the door. Once again, he didn’t make the decision. His body just did it. “Um. I just needed a change. What are you doing here in New Orleans?”

“Work. I dove into the travel nursing game last year, cashing in on the opportunity to make the big bucks and see the world. It’s been hectic but worth it.”

Jake didn’t move toward the couch the way he normally would with a client. “I don’t know if this is a good idea.”

Malachi smirked. “Why? Because we’ve had sex? I would think that would make you uniquely qualified to shrink me.”

Since Malachi fired the first shot, Jake's shoulders squared. "I'm not a shrink and no. Not just because we've had sex, but because we dated for over a year." And had the world's ugliest breakup. And Jake had a restraining order. "That makes this highly unprofessional, at best. I'm not sure why you would even want to seek me out."

Malachi's mouth lifted in one corner. His dark eyes flashed with malice... the way they used to always do before he tore Jake's confidence to shreds. The same sick feeling of not being good enough overcame Jake. Everything he ran from was standing in his living room again. He couldn't breathe.

What's wrong?

Jake took a steadying breath as Aaron's voice stroked his mind.

"Tell me, Jake. Do you still have that ridiculous fear of clowns?"

I need you. The plea rang through Jake's mind with so much fear, he nearly blacked out.

Aaron immediately appeared. "What's wrong, baby?"

Malachi blinked. Then his expression turned thunderous. "No. No interruptions."

Jake's body locked up as if it no longer belonged to him. His gaze moved Aaron's way. *I can't move. I can't talk. Oh my God. What's happening?*

Malachi advanced on them.

Aaron looked confused. He had zapped into the middle of something Jake hadn't warned him might roll into town one day. Of course, Jake couldn't have predicted this.

"I did not turn you so you could play with someone else. You belong to me."

Aaron's eyes widened.

"You do my bidding."

Aaron met his gaze. *Please trust me. I'll be right back.*

You're leaving? Please don't leave me.

Aaron disappeared.

A tear slid down Jake's cheek unchecked.

Malachi laughed. "That's better. You see. That's what happens when you pick a child. They abandon you in your time of need." Malachi brushed his hand down Jake's face, cupping his cheek. Madness swam in his eyes. If Jake was honest with himself, he had always known Malachi was unhinged. He had seen the signs and chose to overlook them. Malachi's broad shoulders and winning personality had won him. Then they had moved in together, and Malachi had immediately become someone else. He had turned sadistic. The being a vampire thing was new, though.

"We have eternity now. You and me. I can make up for all the things I did wrong. You can make up for leaving me. There's no one else out there for you. You know this. No one else will ever really want you. You're really not that exciting or handsome. I'm the only person who sees you and wants you anyhow. That kid is just using you for blood. He doesn't want to accidentally turn any more humans. You're not special to him. Not like you are to me. I can make you feel, though."

Against his will, Jake dropped to his knees. More silent tears rolled down his cheeks. It had been five years. He had thought he was free. Jake had worked on himself. The final step had been moving to New Orleans. He had honestly felt free to love again for the first time. Jake squeezed his eyes closed. He couldn't believe this was happening.

Something hot hit his face and the chokehold keeping him silent disappeared. A loud sob escaped him. Strong arms caught him before he crumpled to the floor.

"It's okay, baby. I've got you."

"Get him out of here. We'll get this cleaned up."

Hands pulled Jake to his feet. Jake finally came back to reality enough to take in the scene. Cosmos and a tall man he didn't recognize stood over a headless Malachi. Jake's stomach heaved.

Aaron covered his eyes. "Don't look." Wind whipped over Jake's skin. He found himself nude and sitting on a bench inside a shower. Aaron turned knobs, firing the water to life. Red mixed with the water, swirling down the drain. Jake couldn't look away. Aaron gently washed him. Shock kept Jake's gaze locked on the blood trailing across the shower floor. The night had started so normally.

"Look at me."

Jake lifted his chin.

Aaron held his stare and washed Jake's face. "You're safe. I would never let anything happen to you."

Jake nodded. His teeth chattered.

Aaron scrubbed Jake's hair. "You're either in shock or you've finally learned to block your thoughts from me. I can't see what happened."

Jake was more thankful for that than he could articulate at the moment. He felt too raw. Humiliated. He stared at Aaron's chin and wished for the ground to swallow him. Jake couldn't tell Aaron he had let an ex beat him and ruin him. He couldn't admit that his past had nearly cost him his life and had stolen his humanity. Jake couldn't say that his ex had pretended to be something as idiotic as a clown when he turned him, because Malachi was that twisted. And Jake, a therapist who should have seen all the warning signs, had fallen in love with and been gaslit by a psychopath until it had nearly destroyed him mentally. Jake didn't know how to say any of that.

"The vampire who turned me came back for me last year." Jake's gaze shot to Aaron's eyes at Aaron's confession. His face looked taut and his gaze turned inward. He kept talking, making Jake want to cover his lips and stop the ugliness. "He kept calling me his 'baby boy.' I felt sick. Before then, I only had nightmares and quick flashes of memories I wasn't sure were real. But when I set eyes on him and heard him call me that, everything rushed back." Aaron seemed to come back to reality. He focused fully on Aaron. "I lied when I said I don't remember the night he turned me. I didn't remember it when I woke up in that abandoned house. But I recall every second of it now and it haunts me constantly. It's okay to be scared of what's out there. I'm terrified of myself. That's another reason I don't like to bite people. I'm not sure what we are is naturally good. What if we have to fight to stay this way?"

Jake took a breath. He realized something monumental. More than one thing, really. First, he loved Aaron. Second, Aaron knew him like no one else ever had. He knew exactly what Jake needed in that moment to keep from drowning, and he gave it to him. When Jake's life had fallen apart, he had wrapped himself in his career. He had used helping people as a crutch and as his armor to survive. Aaron exposed the worst of his insecurities and pain to give Jake something to focus on now other than himself. He was amazing and beautiful and not the least bit broken.

"That was my ex."

Aaron turned away and shut down the water, making Jake wonder what reaction he hoped to hide. When he turned back, he simply looked ready to listen. Jake didn't have much he was ready to tell. Not the gory details anyhow. "He was mentally and physically abusive. We were only together about a year, but it felt like an eternity, and it really messed me up. I never dreamed..." Jake shook his head. A sad smile tugged at his lips. He didn't know how to finish that.

"Of course you didn't. You're not a psychopath." Aaron said the words so easily. He was so sure of Jake. Jake wanted to be certain of him too.

"He said you're only using me for blood because you don't want to accidentally turn any more humans."

Aaron drew back like he had been slapped and turned away. He grabbed a towel and passed it Jake's way. He closed off from Jake so fast, Jake didn't understand what happened.

He wrapped the thick towel around himself like a shield. "What did I do wrong?" Jake hated how he sounded. He felt like he was with Malachi all over again, begging to be loved. To not get shut out.

Aaron turned his way, nude, wet, and seemingly oblivious to all of it. "I'm not Malachi."

Jake winced. It was obvious Aaron could read his thoughts again.

To his surprise, Aaron blinked back tears. "But you won't want me anymore once you know the real me."

God. It had been such an awful night. All Jake wanted was to be held and to forget the nightmare he endured. It didn't look like he would get his wish. "Tell me. It's already been the worst night of my life. Rip everything else away. Tell me Malachi was right. No one will ever love me. I'm boring and not at all handsome. This is just about blood for you while I'm completely in love. Just fucking say it because I'm already on the edge." Even

Jake heard the hysteria in his voice, and he couldn't control it.

Aaron looked at him as if he held his breath. "You love me?"

Jake rolled his eyes. "Don't act like you didn't know. It's not like I can hide anything. You can read my every thought."

"I try to let you have your privacy."

Jake hadn't known that. His throat swelled. Why did Aaron have to keep proving how amazing he was when he wouldn't love Jake back? Jake sniffed. "Yes. I'm in love with you."

Aaron swallowed. He didn't so much as blink. He looked terrified—like he thought Jake might disappear any second. "You know I don't like biting people. Before meeting you, I would put it off until I was starving and sometimes couldn't control the hunger. If you recall, I told you I accidentally turned my step-dad. That's how. He wasn't the only one. I haven't turned anyone since then. Cosmos helped me and then I met you. But I'm not using you. I love you. You're not boring, and you're the sexiest man I have ever set eyes on. I don't know why you'd think otherwise. It'll kill me if you decide you're done with me. That has nothing to do with blood and everything to do with you being the other half of me."

The towel Jake held hit the floor as Jake walked into Aaron's arms. "I'm so sorry. You deserved to do all the typical teenaged rebellions with no real repercussions or someone taking advantage. You didn't deserve anything that happened to you. I'm beyond grateful you feel safe with me and I'm so, so in love with you. You're all I think about anymore."

Aaron held him and kissed his temple. He didn't make Jake feel ridiculous about rambling or coming unglued. It was no wonder Jake loved him. It was inevitable, really.

Aaron had never felt so many conflicting things at once. Knowing Jake loved him meant everything. He worried their age difference would be a point of contention forever since they wouldn't age. But Aaron hated exposing the worst of himself and he absolutely seethed at the thought of anyone harming Jake. He had gone for help because he hadn't known how powerful of a vampire he faced. Cosmos had immediately called for the help of an ancient, Draco. Aaron didn't regret that decision. It had been the smart move. He hadn't been willing to risk Jake's life just so he could be the one who played hero, but damn. Aaron wanted to go back and kill that guy himself. Now that he knew how much that piece of shit had hurt Jake, Aaron felt like a quick death was too good for him.

"Stop."

"What?"

Jake chuckled against his neck. "Your dark thoughts are drowning me."

Aaron tried closing his mind. He hadn't realized he had let his guard down.

I think I'm just in your head now.

"Wow. Look at you, flexing your soulmate muscle."

Jake's hands stroked Aaron's bare stomach. "Look at you, not taking me to bed to hold me."

Aaron swept Jake into his arms.

Jake laughed because Aaron was half his size. Aaron saw it in Jake's head. Jake thought they likely made a funny picture with Aaron carrying him to bed.

A bright smile lit Aaron's face. "You're laughing, but I carried you home like this the night you were attacked."

"Really?" Jake sounded more than a little surprised. "I would've thought you would have zapped me right back to the house with your mind."

Aaron tried arranging his features into some semblance of innocence. "What? And miss my chance at holding you for as long as possible?" Aaron snorted. "I wasn't missing that shit. Drained and covered in clown makeup, you were still sexy as fuck. I had to be the hero and you don't even remember it."

Jake's smile made Aaron's ridiculousness worthwhile. He set Jake on the mattress and climbed into bed next to him before curling against Jake's side.

"I remember waking up and seeing the most gorgeous face I've seen in my life. Surely that counts."

"Who? Cosmos? Someone should kick that guy's ass. It's not fair for him to have it all."

Jake playfully slapped his arm. "You know damn well Cosmos wasn't in the room when I woke up. Will your dad be mad if I'm in your bed? Usually, we stay at my place."

Jake worried too much. It was one of the many things Aaron adored about him. "Dad knows what's going on, but even if he didn't, he wouldn't care if you stayed with us. Everyone here cares about you, angel. You're not alone."

For a moment, Jake held his stare. The absolute silence between them worried Aaron. Even Jake's thoughts went quiet. Then Jake moved, slowly at first. He crawled, forcing Aaron onto his back until he straddled Aaron's body. He never stopped holding Aaron's stare. "I want to be with you."

"You are." Even Aaron heard the confusion in his voice.

Jake shook his head. "Every night, from now on. I want us to be together, but I don't want to rush you and I know I'm making a rash decision after a traumatic experience. But I love you and I know we're meant to be together. Everything you said, the night you taught me to control minds, it's true. One day soon, everything we know now will be dust, but you and I will still be holding on to each other with both hands. I don't think a normal sequence of dating was ever in the cards for us."

"Honestly? I've just been waiting for you to say the word. I've been ready to move at warp speed from the moment we met."

A sweet smile touched Jake's lips. He managed to look shy and sexy at the same time. "Good." He bit his bottom lip and released it. His gaze moved down Aaron's body. "Thank you for taking care of me and coming the instant I called. I don't know what would've happened if you wouldn't have come."

Aaron had a bad feeling he knew, and it would never happen on his watch. "I love you. Nothing in this world could ever stop me from coming when you call."

"I love you too."

The seriousness in Jake's voice couldn't be ignored. Everything about this was real. Aaron squeezed Jake's ass and pulled him closer, causing a delicious friction between them. He hadn't thought. The move had been out of habit. "Sorry. You don't need me pawing at you tonight."

"Yes, I do."

Jake's immediate response had too much power behind it for Aaron to argue. It was obvious Jake knew his mind. Still, Aaron moved slowly as he drew Jake down for a kiss. When their lips met, they shared each other's air for a moment before Jake deepened their kiss. As their tongues stroked, Jake rocked himself forward, letting their bodies massage their cocks together. Aaron grew longer and harder by the second. He had been trying to ignore the sexy nude body straddling him so he could focus on caring for Jake. With the green light given, Aaron held two handfuls of ass again and controlled the pace.

It never took much for Jake to get him hot. In no time, Aaron moaned uncontrollably and panted for air. His fangs grew. The need for blood mixed with his drive to come. He no longer knew which longing drove him the most insane.

"Bite me. Please," Jake begged. "I need your fangs buried in my throat, sucking me while I blow. Take everything."

Aaron buried his face in the crook of Jake's neck. His delicious scent overcame Aaron. Aaron struck. His fangs sank into Jake's flesh. Jake shot cum all over Aaron's dick and stomach. An orgasm tore through Aaron. He moaned as he sucked Jake's blood. The greatest flavor he ever tasted filled his mouth as his body writhed beneath Jake. Pleasure rocked him to his soul. He had to force himself to retract his fangs and seal the wound, but he kept sucking, leaving a hickey behind. It would heal almost instantly too, but Aaron knew he had marked Jake's skin, if only temporarily. He needed to have some way for the world to see Jake belonged to him. It made him almost insane how badly he wanted to publicly take Jake off the market. He felt almost insanely possessive with the combined cum coating his skin and Jake's blood pumping through his veins.

How about you mark your territory with a ring?

As the words brushed Aaron's brain, Aaron finally took a calming breath. Yes.

That was the answer. Even though they would outlive every human concept of marriage, that didn't mean Aaron didn't want it. In fact, he wouldn't rest easy again until there was a ring on Jake's finger.

"And one on yours too."

Aaron kissed the tip of Jake's nose. "Of course." He had been off the market since the first moment he set eyes on Jake... if he had ever really been on the market at all. Aaron felt like he had always been waiting for Jake. His other half. His better half. The best part of his world.

CHAPTER FIVE

SIX MONTHS OF BEING a vampire seemed to frustrate Jake some days. While most supernatural beings developed their own version of a special power pretty early on, Jake didn't have an easy time finding a specific thing he excelled at. Aaron didn't know how to help except to ask the least intimidating vampire he knew to work with him. Tate was married to one of the oldest and most powerful living vampires, Draco, but he was a Little. He was as sweet as they came.

Aaron sat in the corner and watched as they brainstormed possible powers. "Can you fly? Have you tried becoming a bat?"

Jake shook his head. "Aaron said you can do that and so can a lot of other vampires, but I can't. I levitated a little once, but then I fell. But I've heard you're a pretty dang cute sky puppy."

"Oooh, I like you." Tate beamed. He was adorable in human form too, with his blond curls and big green eyes. Tate shifted his teddy bear from one hip to the other while looking thoughtful. "Hmmm. We've established no batting out and no traveling through time and space like Draco and Aaron. Of course, that's a super rare talent. Usually, only ancients can do that."

Aaron's eyebrows shot up. He hadn't known that.

Jake looked his way and winked. He could feel Jake's pride. Jake went back to facing Tate. It was obvious he didn't want Tate to think he wasn't paying attention.

Tate chewed his bottom lip. He looked stumped.

Jake's shoulders fell.

Aaron winced. He knew Jake was about to throw in the towel. "Maybe you two should feed before it gets too late. That might help you think clearer. I could zap us over to The Rabbit Hole. You could grab a bite, and then I could zap us right back."

Tate's eyes widened. He hugged his bear to his chest. "I only drink from Draco. Even so, no. The Rabbit Hole is where I was turned. I couldn't—" He looked panicked.

Aaron felt like an ass for suggesting something that obviously spiked a terrible memory in Tate.

Jake took Tate's hand. "It's okay. If you're up to sharing what happened that night, sometimes just saying the words to people you trust can take away the power of a memory."

Tate's body visibly relaxed. He held Jake's stare. Aaron expected him to blow off the suggestion, but he didn't. "I went there like this." He nodded toward the way he was dressed: footed pajamas. "It didn't seem like a big deal. The Rabbit Hole is supposed to be for people like me. Before I made it inside the playpen for Littles, this man stopped me. He hurt me." Tate whispered the last words with tears welling in his eyes. Aaron's chest tightened. His throat swelled. The idea of anyone hurting someone as sweet as Tate was sickening. Then Tate blinked. His face cleared. "How did you do that?"

Jake looked confused. "What?"

Tate nodded toward their joined hands. "I told you my story, and you took away the emotion attached to it. One second, I felt everything from that night. The next, it was like that night was only a picture in my head with no feelings attached any longer. I felt the emotions draining from me—like they were sliding down my arm and into you. It was you. You took them." A smile exploded across Tate's face. "Oh, my God. You're a healer. That's your power. You drain people's negative energy—like an emotional vampire."

Jake looked between them. "What?"

Aaron thought back to finally telling Jake he remembered everything about his attack. Tate was right. Jake had taken the hurt from the memory and now it was just a memory with no emotion attached. Aaron had thought he had been healed because Jake loved him, but Tate's explanation made more sense. He should still feel something when he thought about that night, but he didn't.

Jake covered his mouth, obviously listening to Aaron's thoughts.

Tate bounced on his toes and clapped. "You'll be swimming in supernatural business. Night dwellers will come from around the globe for your services. I have to go tell Draco so he can start spreading the word. You're about to be the most sought-after therapist in the world."

Jake kept looking between them with his hands covering his mouth. As they looked on, Tate turned into a bat. Jake dropped his hands. "Awww. Holy shit. You are freaking adorable as hell. Can I cuddle you for a second before you go?"

Tate flew into Jake's hands and let Jake nuzzle him before moving toward the door.

Aaron opened it so he could fly into the night. "Thank you for your help."

Tate let out a little squeak before disappearing.

Aaron closed the door and turned Jake's way. The way Jake beamed had Aaron's chest swelling with pride. "Damn. Every day, you get a little farther out of my league. Tell me again why you love me?"

Jake rolled his eyes. "Please? Weren't you listening? You have powers only seen in ancients. My husband has that," Jake said, poking himself in the chest.

Aaron couldn't stop smiling as he wrapped his arms around Jake's waist.

Jake looked thoughtful. "All this has me thinking, what are your dads' powers? I've never noticed or thought to ask."

Aaron nearly groaned at the question. "Well, Cosmos is ten times stronger and faster than even the typical vampire, which is like ridiculously fast and strong. But he was a fitness buff before turning, so that's not surprising, I guess." Aaron hesitated.

Jake wasn't having it. "And Vega?"

Aaron sighed. "Apparently, he has sexual allure."

A surprised and uncomfortable-sounding chuckle escaped Jake. "What?"

Aaron nodded. "Men and women won't leave him alone. He can get anything he wants anywhere he goes now. People flirt with him outrageously and just give him everything for free. I don't think anything changed between Cosmos and him. Cosmos always pawed at him like he was dying of thirst, and Dad was the last drop of water on earth, but still. It's a bit horrifying."

Jake snorted. His snort became a full-blown laugh. He covered his mouth. "I'm sorry." He visibly fought to stop, only to end up laughing harder. Jake tried talking through his chuckles. "I'm just picturing you trying to ignore Cosmos tearing off your dad's clothes constantly. I can't get the image out of my head."

Aaron scooped Jake off his feet and headed for the bedroom. "I'll teach you to picture my dads in inappropriate situations." He stamped his way toward the bed. "Now I have to give you new images."

"Oops." Jake didn't sound the least bit contrite. In fact, he sounded as if his plan had come to fruition, and Aaron was about to give him exactly what he wanted. That was fine. As always, they were on the same page. They were both bent on happiness and an eternity together. It was enough to almost make Aaron grateful for the terrible things that led them here. He would do it all again if it meant he ended up right here with the love of his life. Aaron would do anything for their happy ending. They were worth it.

Please consider leaving a review at the retailer where you purchased this book. Reviews really help with a book's visibility, which allows me to continue writing more stories. Thank you, Charity.

ABOUT THE AUTHOR

CHARITY PARKERSON IS AN award-winning and multi-published author with several companies. Born with no filter from her brain to her mouth, she decided to take this odd quirk and insert it in her characters. One of her greatest loves is writing morally gray characters. You'll find them scattered throughout her hundreds of titles.

*Eight-time Readers' Favorite Award Winner

*2015 Passionate Plume Award Finalist

*2013 Reviewers' Choice Award Winner

*2012 ARRA Finalist for Favorite Paranormal Romance

*Five-time winner of The Mistress of the Darkpath

Connect with her online:

*Sign up for her newsletter: https://sendfox.com/charityparkerson

*Join her readers' group on Facebook: http://bit.ly/CharitysTribe

*Website: https://www.charityparkerson.com

*A list of her social media accounts and giveaways all in one place: http://hy.page/charityparkerson

www.ingramcontent.com/pod-product-compliance
Lightning Source LLC
Chambersburg PA
CBHW052007220626
47052CB00004B/1131

* 9 7 8 1 9 5 9 5 7 6 1 4 3 *